A story of pond life

frog

Written by Ruth Thomson
Illustrated by Martin Ursell

PUBLISHED BY THE READER'S DIGEST ASSOCIATION LIMITED
IN CONJUNCTION WITH mothercare® LIMITED

Summer was almost over.
High above the pond,
the swallows were gathering
for their flight to the sun.

Fergus and Bessie sat on a lily pad
watching the swallows
and making the most of the sunshine.
"Hasn't time gone quickly?"
said Fergus. "I can remember
when we were only tadpoles."
"I can remember," said Bessie,
"the very day we hatched."
"A likely story," croaked Fergus.

"I can, I can," said Bessie.
"There were thousands of us.
The day we hatched,
the pond was black with tadpoles.

I can remember clinging
to some water-weed
and looking around.
The pond seemed enormous."

"There was so much to see,"
said Fergus. "I spent days
and days wriggling about
exploring the pond."
"So did I," said Bessie,
"and whenever I felt hungry,
I nibbled at some water-weed.

But not everyone was friendly.
I was always on the look-out
for hungry beetles and fish."
"We were lucky to escape,"
agreed Fergus.

"Wasn't it fun to grow so fast,"
said Bessie, quickly changing
the subject.

"Bigger,

and bigger,

and bigger every day."

"It was even more amazing
to grow legs," interrupted Fergus.

"First back ones,

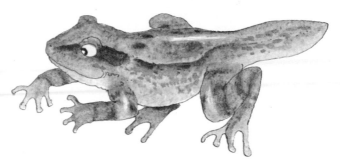

then front ones."

"I liked my new strong jaws as well," said Fergus.

"Me too," replied Bessie, remembering lovely meals of worms and grubs.

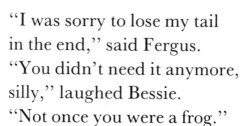

"I was sorry to lose my tail
in the end," said Fergus.
"You didn't need it anymore,
silly," laughed Bessie.
"Not once you were a frog."

"Do you remember the first time
you hopped on to dry land?"
"I certainly do," said Fergus.
"I jumped right into a clump
of marsh marigolds."

"That's nothing," said Bessie,
"I jumped right over the rushes."

"I found a wonderful place
to live," Fergus went on,
"among some damp, smelly leaves
under a tree."

"I found a better place than that,"
said Bessie, "under a smooth stone
hidden by the reeds."

Bessie was beginning to annoy
Fergus. She was so boastful.
"I'll show her," he muttered.
He took a deep breath.
"Do you know," Fergus began,
"that once I sat under my tree
all day and caught
a wriggly worm . . .

two slimy slugs,

three slow snails,

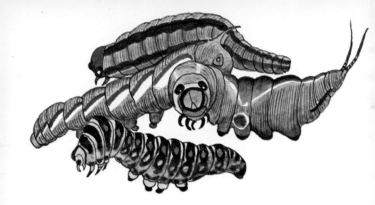

four juicy caterpillars,

five green grasshoppers,

ten fat beetles,

and two dozen flies?"

"That's nothing," said Bessie,
"Why, I sat on my stone one day
and caught a darting damselfly . . .

two black spiders,

three busy bumblebees,

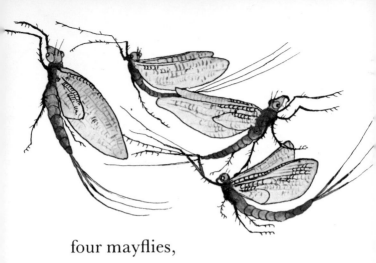

four mayflies,

five beautiful butterflies,

twenty fat beetles

and *three dozen* flies!''

"Do you know," said Fergus quickly,
not to be outdone,
"I had three narrow escapes
all in a row.
One morning a sneaky grass snake
slithered right past my nose.

The next day,
a sharp-eyed heron
made a grab for me.

The day after that,
I had to make a quick getaway
from a big brown rat."

"Pooh, pooh," said Bessie,
"That's nothing at all.
I had three narrow escapes
all in one evening.

"First of all,
an enormous owl came swooping
down from the sky.
I dived into the pond to escape
and came face to face with . . .

a fearsome pike
lurking in the reeds.
I leaped back on the shore
and almost bumped into . . .

a hungry hedgehog
snuffling around for food.
I was quite worn out
after that, I can tell you."

Fergus didn't know
quite what to say.
He thought quickly.
"Do you know," he said,
"that whenever there's a rainstorm
I come out and leap
higher than the grass?"

"That's nothing," said Bessie,
I've leaped higher than the moon."
Fergus knew that couldn't be true,
but he didn't say anything.

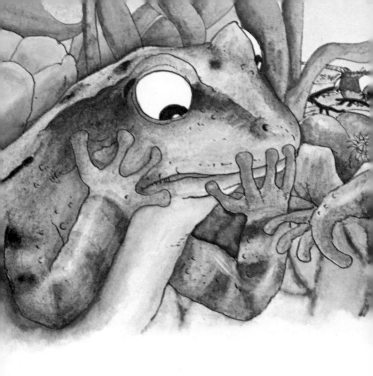

After a long silence, Fergus said,
"I've found a wonderful hole
to sleep in for the winter."
Bessie turned to look at him.

"Yes," said Fergus smugly.
"When the wind blows
and the pond freezes
and the snow falls, I'll be warm
and cosy."

Bessie hadn't found a hole.
She thought about what Fergus said
and gave a shiver.
In a small voice, she said,
"Do you think I could share it
with you?"
"Of course," said Fergus,
feeling extra pleased with himself.
"Come and have a look at it."
Bessie thought it was
a splendid hole.

When the days started
getting shorter,
the two frogs crept into the hole
and huddled together.
Outside, a cold wind blew.
The leaves fell off the trees
and the sun scarcely shone.

Winter came.
Snow fell on the fields
and the ditches.
The pond froze.
Hungry ducks slithered
over the ice looking for food.

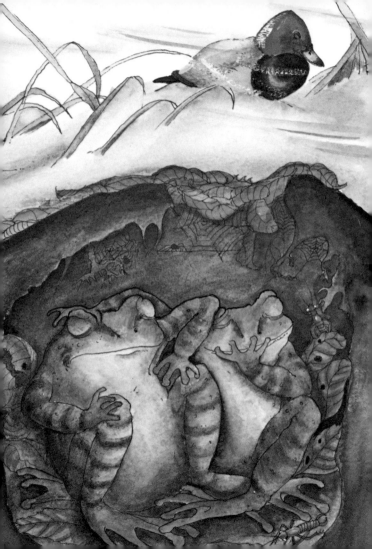

The two frogs slept on and on
in their snug little hole.
They didn't even wake up
for Christmas.

They woke up
only when the snow had melted
and the buds were on the trees.
"See you here next year,"
said Fergus, as he leaped off
to find some food.
"Only if I don't find
a better sort of hole,"
said Bessie leap-frogging over him,
down to the pond.

MY NATURE LIBRARY

First Edition Copyright © 1982
The Reader's Digest Association
Limited,
25 Berkeley Square, London W1X 6AB
Reprinted 1985

mothercare® is the registered
trademark of Mothercare Limited,
Watford, Herts, England

Phototypeset by Tradespools Limited
Frome, Somerset.
Printed in Hong Kong